THE NAUGHTIEST UNICORN

AT CHRISTMAS

PIP BIRD

ILLUSTRATED BY DAVID O'CONNELL

EGMONT

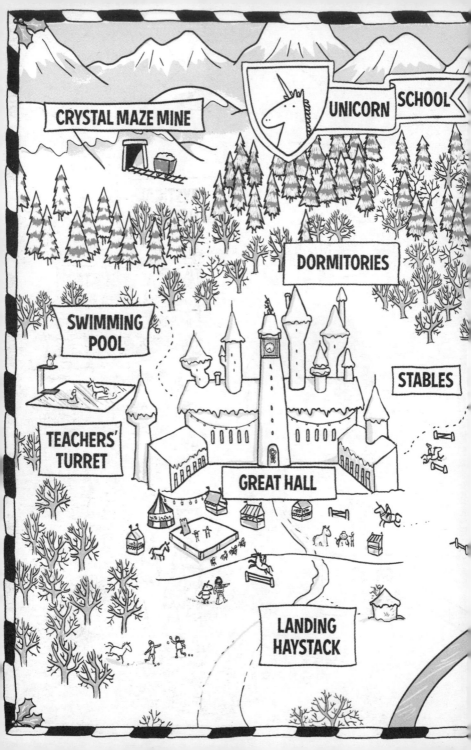

MYSTICAL
DANGER CLIFF

FEARSOME
FOREST

GLITTER
GLADE

MEADOW

GRAND
PADDOCK

# Contents

CHAPTER ONE
Snow Much Fun!

'Look, there's some snow!' cried Mira excitedly as she leapt out of the car in the leisure-centre car park.

Her sister Rani stepped out of the car and peered over, wrinkling her nose. 'That,' she said, 'is *slush*.'

Mira bent closer to the small pile of snow, which was a *bit* slushy. And grey. 'There's definitely some specks of white,' she said. She had been so excited when she looked out of the window the night before and saw snowflakes falling. Mira's mum and dad said it wouldn't settle, but Mira was *sure* that

she could find some to play with. It was the week before Christmas, and she had spent *days* planning fun things to do, ALL of which involved snow.

'You couldn't even get a snowball out of that,' said Rani, as Mira reached towards the slushy puddle.

'Time to go!' said their mum quickly. 'You don't want to be late for Unicorn School.'

And Mum was right – Mira absolutely did not want to be late for Unicorn School! Unicorn School was the best thing ever. You were paired up with your UBFF (Unicorn Best Friend Forever) and you went on quests and magical adventures. And even the ordinary lessons were a million

UBFFs 4 EVER

per cent better than the ones at normal school because the unicorns were there!

Mira, Rani and Mum walked over to the corner of the car park, where the magic portal to Unicorn School lay hidden behind some bushes. There was a queue of children waiting for their turn to go through. Everyone was wearing brightly-coloured festive jumpers.

Christmas was Mira's *favourite* time of year. She loved seeing her breath in the chilly air, the way trees sparkled with frost and being cosy inside with a mug of hot chocolate. (She had a feeling that her greedy unicorn, Dave, would enjoy the hot chocolate, too.)

Mira quickly looked through her school bag

3

to make sure that she had everything. There were LOTS of pairs of thick woolly socks (added by her mum), treats for Dave, her pencil case, and something very important: *The Legend of the Snow Unicorn.*

Every year at Christmas time, Class Red performed a play of *The Legend of the Snow Unicorn,* and before they went home at the end of the last visit their teacher, Miss Glitterhorn, had given them each a script to learn. Mira knew the whole thing off by heart and she was

secretly hoping that she and Dave would get the lead roles of Snow Unicorn and Snow Child!

It was nearly time to go

4

through the portal and Rani said Mum had to
go where the other parents were all standing
huddled together, so Mum gave them each a hug
and a kiss and told them for about the eightieth
time to wrap up warm.

'Will there be snow at Unicorn School?'
Mira asked her sister.

'Only if you do the snow dance,' said Rani.

'What's the snow dance?' said Mira.

Rani sighed. 'It's quite difficult. Only Class
Yellow can do it. You probably won't manage it.'

Mira narrowed her eyes. She didn't always
believe the things her sister told her, but she also
didn't want to take any chances. Especially when
it came to unicorn stuff. Rani had been at school

for longer than Mira and had LOTS of medals, as she always liked to remind Mira.

'Just tell me how to do the snow dance,' she said.

'Fine!' said Rani. 'You have to squat like a frog and then stomp around, waving your hands in the air and grunting.'

Mira shuffled into position.

'Make sure you close your eyes and really get into it,' said Rani.

Mira started doing the snow dance. It was a bit slippy and slidey on the slushy floor, but the dance wasn't hard at all – she didn't know what Rani was on about.

'Mira . . .?'

Mira opened her eyes. Her friend Darcy

was there, looking concerned. Lots of the other

children were backing away.

'I'm doing the snow dance,' said Mira.

'Oh. I thought you really needed the loo.'

Darcy moved her wheelchair next to Mira in

the magic portal queue and they did their usual

high-five greeting. Darcy was wearing a coat with

rainbow stripes and a matching hat.

'Is Raheem here yet?' said Mira. She wondered if the snow dance was more powerful if more people did it.

Darcy pointed over to the bike racks, where Raheem was doing a strange sort of hop. 'He's been doing that for a while. And before that he was reading a story about teddy bears out loud.' She paused. '*Everyone's* being weird today.'

There was a small girl clinging to Raheem's leg. She must be his little sister, Mira thought. Raheem's dad was there, trying to untangle them as the girl cried loudly.

'He's only going away for a little bit, Tia!' said Raheem's dad.

The girl wailed even more. 'I want to go with

you!' she sobbed.

Raheem looked at his dad.

'You can't, Tia sweetheart,' said Raheem's dad.

The little girl clung to Raheem's leg even tighter and sobbed even louder.

Darcy held out a biscuit and whistled. 'Tia! Come on!' She waved the biscuit and clicked her fingers.

Tia stopped crying for a second and gave Darcy a strange look, before bursting into loud sobs again.

Darcy shrugged. 'It works with my dog,' she said.

They watched as Raheem continued to struggle. Then Mira had an idea.

'Look!' she shouted. 'One of the unicorns has come through the magic portal and into the car park!'

Everyone in the car park turned to look where Mira was pointing, including Raheem's little sister. Mira and Darcy grabbed Raheem and dragged him towards the magic portal, pushing past the queue of children.

'Love you, Tia! Love you, Dad!' Raheem called
back, but his dad was looking around worriedly
for the escaped unicorn.

They reached the clump of bushes.

Raheem didn't have the chance to be nervous
going through the magic portal. Mira and Darcy
were still holding on to his arms, and they pulled
him through the entrance.

Mira would *never* get used to the magic portal
– the way it sucked you through, and then
zoomed you along the rainbow like you were
on a rollercoaster but a million times faster and
not wearing safety belts. Mira gripped her
friends' hands and the exciting feeling grew in
her chest until she thought she might burst.

Rainbow colours and sparkly stars flew past them – and Mira was sure that this time, she could see flurries of snowflakes . . .

They all arrived with a thud on the landing haystack. Mira peered around and blinked.

'THE SNOW DANCE WORKED!' she yelled.

CHAPTER TWO
A Winter Wonderland

The snow was more perfect than any snow Mira had ever seen. It covered the whole paddock in a thick, powdery blanket that glittered and sparkled. Mira wondered if maybe unicorn snow was a little bit magical.

Further away Mira could see the snow-topped turrets of the Unicorn School buildings and the white-tipped trees of the Fearsome Forest.

Mira jumped down from the haystack. The perfect snow made the perfect crunching sound under her snow boots. She could see lots

13

of different footprints leading away from the landing haystack and – much more excitingly – hoofprints!

Darcy wheeled down the ramp from the haystack to where her unicorn, Star, was waiting for her in a bright rainbow snow coat with a rainbow hat over her ears.

'OMG, we match!' said Darcy, throwing her arms around Star.

They started making their way across the paddock. All around them children and their unicorns were playing in the snow. Some were having snowball fights, while others were taking it in turns to slide down a little hill in the corner of the paddock. They were just walking past a Class Yellow boy and his unicorn making a snowman, when they heard a thundering sound and saw a blur of blue against the white. Raheem's unicorn, Brave, came galloping towards them. Brave was the biggest unicorn at Unicorn School, and the thundering of his hooves made the ground shake.

'Watch out for my snowman!' cried the boy, and his unicorn snorted in agreement.

Brave skidded to a halt. The snowman wobbled but stayed standing. Then Brave stomped his hoof. A big pile of snow slid from a tree branch, knocking off the snowman's head and completely burying Raheem.

As they all dug Raheem out, Mira looked around. 'Can anyone see Dave?' she said.

Star snorted and pointed across the paddock with her horn.

'He's wrestling Miss Glitterhorn,' said Darcy.

'He's . . . what?' said Mira.

In the corner of the paddock by the gate was their class teacher, Miss Glitterhorn. She was indeed wrestling with a unicorn. And that unicorn was the plumpest, naughtiest unicorn at Unicorn School – Dave!

When they got a bit closer, Mira realised that Miss Glitterhorn was actually trying to wrap a long, rainbow scarf around Dave, but he kept wriggling out of the teacher's grip.

'You have to wrap up warm, Dave!' said Miss Glitterhorn.

Mira thought they must have been doing this for a long time as Miss Glitterhorn looked very annoyed and sweaty, even though it was a cold day. But Mira was mostly thinking about how great it was to see her UBFF.

'Dave!' she called out, waving excitedly to him.

Dave looked up from his wriggling. Miss Glitterhorn looked up too and stopped holding on to him. Dave bolted and galloped towards Mira, snorting happily as he went. The long scarf trailed behind him through the snow as he got to the top of a little hill in the paddock.

'Running on snow is a NO!' yelped Raheem.

Sure enough, the scarf tangled in Dave's hooves and he tripped. He tumbled into a forward roll. And then he kept rolling.

'What goes RAINBOW *thump*, RAINBOW *thump*, RAINBOW *thump*, RAINBOW *thump*?' said Darcy.

The others didn't answer as they watched the tumbling unicorn.

'Dave rolling down a hill!' finished Darcy.

'I don't think he's going to stop!' cried Raheem, as Dave continued to roll towards them.

They all jumped to the side as the Dave snowball rolled straight through where they'd been standing, showering everyone in white fluff. He smashed right into the headless snowman and finally came to a stop.

'For goodness' sake!' said the boy.

'Dave!' cried Mira as the others brushed snow out of their hair and manes. The Class Yellow boy started rebuilding his snowman, muttering and giving them evil glares.

Dave trotted over and gave a big shake, like a wet dog, showering them all in snow again. Mira gave her UBFF a big unicorn hug. Dave nuzzled her face and snorted, which tickled and made Mira laugh. And then the whole gang went round doing high fives (and hoof fives for the unicorns).

'This is going to be the best week-before-Christmas ever!' said Mira.

'Yeah!' said Darcy and Raheem together.

Star gave a loud whinny.

22

Brave stamped his hoof again, dislodging a fresh batch of snow on to Raheem's head.

'What do you think, Dave?' said Mira.

Dave snorted, frowned, and did a massive, frozen poo.

They all stared at it in wonder.

'It's perfectly round,' said Raheem. 'Like a football or a globe or something.'

Brave wrinkled his nose.

'Well done, Dave!' said Mira, grinning.

'I mean, it is still a poo,' said Darcy. 'Let's not get carried away.'

The bell in the clocktower chimed. It was time to go to assembly. Mira, Darcy, Raheem, Star, Brave and Dave started making their way across

the rest of the paddock and towards the Unicorn School building.

Mira turned back, realising she needed to find the poo shovel and clean up after Dave. But the poo had gone! Mira was confused for a second, until she noticed that the boy from Class Yellow had finished his snowman. The snowman's head was a perfectly round, frozen poo.

'Er . . .' said Raheem.

'Should we say something?' said Mira.

Darcy shook her head. 'The damage is done,' she said.

∪∪∪

Mira, Raheem and Darcy sat in the gallery of the Great Hall, which was a bit like an indoor

riding school with a stage at one end. Today the hall looked extra special. Boughs of holly and garlands of tinsel covered the walls, candles hung flickering from the ceiling, and the floor sparkled with a layer of glittering snow. The children had kept their coats on, and most of the unicorns were wearing brightly coloured Christmas jumpers with woolly hats perched on their heads.

A hush descended on the hall. Something small and strangely fluffy was climbing on to the stage.

'It's a BEAR!' shouted Darcy.

The gallery burst into shrieking and two unicorns bolted out of the doors.

'It's just Madame Shetland wearing a furry coat and hat,' said Raheem.

'Oh,' said Darcy.

The teachers ran around getting children and unicorns back in their seats. 'Darcy! See me after assembly!' shouted Miss Glitterhorn as she chased after a girl from Class Green.

Eventually they managed to calm everyone down, and Madame Shetland began the assembly.

'Now this is a very special time at Unicorn School,' she said. 'Our Snow Unicorn celebrations will soon be underway.'

Madame Shetland told them that every class would contribute something to the celebrations. Then she talked them through what each class would do, starting with the oldest – Class Violet – who would be making a Snow Unicorn ice sculpture.

Mira already knew what her class would be doing. But she couldn't wait for the head teacher to tell them about it.

'Isn't this your favourite time of the year,

Dave?' Mira whispered. She popped her woolly hat on his horn, thinking he was looking a bit chilly. Dave snorted. The horn-hat flew up into the air, floated down towards a unicorn standing nearby, and landed on its bum.

'And last but certainly not least,' continued Madame Shetland, 'Class Red will round off the Snow Unicorn celebrations by performing the traditional festive play: *The Legend of the Snow Unicorn.*'

Mira let out a squeal, which made Raheem yelp and Dave fart with surprise.

'Quiet please,' said Madame Shetland. 'As you know, this special story tells how the bond between unicorn and child came to be.

This is *such* a special event that we invite parents and guardians along to watch. So I expect you and your UBFFs to be on your best behaviour – to give it your absolute all, and make us proud.'

Mira remembered when her parents had gone to see her sister in the Christmas play. Rani had been playing the lead role, of course. Mira had begged them to take her too, but it was parents and guardians only.

'The auditions will take place right after assembly,' continued Madame Shetland. 'And remember, there will be a special prize for the most inspiring performance: the Star of the Show medal.'

Mira gripped her chair. A special medal! Now

she HAD to get the lead role. 'Dave, I know we can do it!' she whispered to her unicorn.

Dave burped.

'That would be a week-before-Christmas miracle,' hissed Rani from the row behind.

Mira opened her mouth to reply but Madame Shetland gave them both a Look. 'And finally,' she said. 'After the play is performed, you will all leave your special Christmas wishes for the Snow Unicorn. And, if you are very lucky and those wishes come from the goodness of your heart, perhaps the Snow Unicorn might appear and make those wishes come true.' The head teacher clapped her hands. 'Now, time for your first lessons.'

As the children filed out, the hall buzzed as they all whispered about their wishes.

'I'm going to wish for EVERLASTING CHOCOLATE,' said Flo.

Dave whinnied loudly in approval.

'I'm going to wish I was a unicorn!' said Seb. Seb's unicorn, Firework, who had a rainbow mane and wore shades, gave an approving snort.

'I'm going to wish I can FLY!' said Freya.

'I'm going to wish to be FAMOUS,' said Darcy. 'What about you, Raheem?'

'I don't know yet,' said Raheem. 'I need to think about it and make a list of all the possible options.'

Mira knew what *her* wish was going to be:
to win the Star of the Show medal!

'Come on, Dave,' she said. 'We need to spend
EVERY SPARE MOMENT learning our lines!'

CHAPTER THREE
The Realm of the Theatre...

A little while later, Class Red stood nervously in the corridor, waiting to audition for the play. Mira really, really hoped that she and Dave could play the lead roles: Snow Unicorn and Snow Child.

'Wouldn't it be amazing to play the role of the first EVER UBFFs, Dave?' she said.

Dave gave a weird, muffled snort. Mira saw that he had his head in her school bag.

'Dave!' Mira grabbed her bag and looked inside. He had bitten a chunk out of her script.

'It's lucky that I've learned the lines for every part!' She slipped Dave a mini doughnut, which he slurped up happily. 'And you can have the rest of them if you help me ace this audition.'

Dave's eyes went wide, and then he started busily wiping the spit off Mira's script with his hooves.

'You learned ALL the lines?' said Raheem, sounding impressed. 'The main part has loads!'

'It didn't take me too long,' said Mira. 'I just read it twenty-nine times! And actually, the narrator has the most lines of all.'

Raheem looked at his own script, which was looking a bit dog-eared. 'I've been looking through for parts that don't have any lines so I could just mime,' he said worriedly.

'You may now enter my realm,' called a voice from inside the classroom.

The children all filed in. Mira saw that the Classroom 7 sign had a bit of paper stuck over it which read REALM OF THE THEATRE. All the chairs and desks had been moved to the side, and in the middle of the room stood a very tall woman dressed head to toe in purple.

'I am Ms Dazzleflank' she boomed. 'When the mood takes you, Class Red, be at one with the floor.'

Class Red stared at her.

'Sit down,' said Ms Dazzleflank.

They sat down.

'ACTING!' Ms Dazzleflank shouted, making them all jump. 'Acting is NOT about learning lines.'

Mira felt a pang of disappointment and gripped her script. Raheem raised his eyebrows hopefully. Darcy looked delighted. She'd told Mira and Raheem earlier that she hadn't read any of the script 'because it looked quite long'.

'ACTING,' shouted Ms Dazzleflank, 'is about FEELING the words take hold of you. Let them BURST forth and gush out of you like a waterfall.'

Class Red all looked at each other. Flo put up her hand.

Ms Dazzleflank shut her eyes, held up her arms and said, 'Speak!'

'Um,' said Flo. 'Just to check – are we supposed to wet ourselves?'

'NO,' said Ms Dazzleflank. 'It was a metaphor. Now repeat after me: there is a fountain in my MIND.'

'There is a fountain in my mind,' chorused the class.

'There is a waterfall in my CHEST,' said Ms Dazzleflank.

'There is a waterfall in my chest,' repeated the class.

'There is a . . . unicorn in your bag?' said Ms Dazzleflank.

'There is a . . . unicorn in your bag,' said the class all together.

'No, I mean, you – that girl there. There's a unicorn in your bag,' said Ms Dazzleflank,

40

pointing at Flo.

'No, I mean, you – that girl there. There's a unicorn in your bag,' said the class.

'For goodness' sake,' said Ms Dazzleflank.

'For goodness' sake,' said the class.

Eventually Ms Dazzleflank strode over to where Flo was sitting – and where Dave stood with his head buried in a school bag, making suspicious munching sounds.

MMUUNNNCHH MMUUNNNCHH MMUUNNNCHH

'Dave!' Mira grabbed the school bag and pulled it off his head. Dave looked around in surprise but continued to chew.

'He's eaten your whole script! I'm so sorry,

41

Flo!' said Mira. 'I think he was trying to get to the snacks.'

Dave coughed and spat something on to the ground, which Flo picked up. It was two tiny scraps of paper – all that was left of her script. One said 'I'm so lonely' and the other said 'Look at the sn'.

'You can use mine,' said Mira, going back to her bag to get her script.

'Don't worry. These are great!' said Flo,

grinning and holding up the pieces of paper.

'Now,' said Ms Dazzleflank, 'before we audition, we will get a SENSE of the world of the play. What is this story? How does it FEEL? What does it TASTE like? Can I have a volunteer to open that magical door?'

The class all looked at each other again.

'Can someone give a brief summary of what happens in the play,' said Ms Dazzleflank.

'I can! I can!' said Mira, leaping to her feet. 'I can tell the whole story with all the details and everything.'

'Details are wonderful. But let's keep it brief,' said Ms Dazzleflank, glancing at her watch. But Mira had already begun.

'Once upon a time,' said Mira, 'there was a girl who lived in a cottage in the woods and her life was quite ordinary and boring, and more than anything she wished she could swap lives with the Prince who lived next door in a massive castle, because the Prince had EVERYTHING you could ever want, like his favourite food any time he liked, and the best toys that he just threw away at the end of the day and got new ones in the morning. And seventy million horses.'

'He can't have had that many horses. That's stupid,' said Jake, who always liked to prove he knew the most about everything.

'And EIGHTY million horses,' continued Mira, glaring at Jake. 'And one day it was winter, and

44

it was snowing loads. And the Girl was standing
outside the castle getting snowed on and being
sad and staring up at the Prince's bedroom
window –'

'Perhaps we could speed up – I only have this
room for an hour,' said Ms Dazzleflank.

Mira talked faster. 'And then she heard a voice
calling to her . . . "Don't be sad, little girl!" And
she turned round and there was this weird scabby
old donkey, and she was like, "WHAT?! Did that
donkey just talk?" And the Donkey said, "I was
wondering why you are so sad?" And the Girl
told him all about how she wished she could
swap lives with the Prince. And it turned out that
the Donkey was magic and could grant WISHES!'

'Yay!' shouted Flo.

'And so the Donkey said the Girl could have ONE WISH, and the Girl knew she was definitely going to wish to swap lives with the Prince. But the Donkey said you should have a think about it. And then the Donkey MELTED into the air!'

There was a GASP from the class.

'We'll have to leave it there,' said Ms
Dazzleflank, clapping her hands.

'But we didn't even get to the bit where the
Snow Unicorn appears!' said Seb.

'We need to start the auditions!' said Ms
Dazzleflank.

'*Everyone* knows what happens,' said Jake.
'The Girl makes her wish, the weird, scabby
old Donkey turns into the Snow Unicorn, they
become UBFFs and they all sing Jingle Horns.'

Mira sat back down in her place in the circle.
Telling the story had got her even more excited
about being in the play. She wanted the main part
(and the medal) more than ANYTHING!

Darcy was up first. She wheeled to the middle of the circle with her unicorn, Star, trotting by her side.

'And which role will you be auditioning for?' asked Ms Dazzleflank.

'Anything except the main one,' said Darcy.

The class murmured in surprise.

'Star doesn't want to be a weird scabby old donkey for most of the play and I respect that,' Darcy explained.

'In your own time,' said Ms Dazzleflank. 'Don't you need a script?'

'Oh, I'm going to let the words drain out of my body or whatever you said,' Darcy told her.

Darcy and Star took a bow. And then Darcy

sang a medley of her favourite Disney songs –
with accompanying dance moves – while Star
clapped her hooves and beatboxed.

One by one they all went to the middle of
the circle. A couple of people wanted to be the
main role, and some didn't mind what they were.
Jake said he wanted to be the Prince, because
the Prince was obviously the coolest, and
Freya said she'd also quite like to be the Prince.
Raheem said he'd like to be the smallest role and
performed a short mime.

Mira thought her audition went pretty well.
Dave was on his best behaviour, although he
did keep stopping and nudging Mira to see if
he could have his mini doughnuts yet.

Ms Dazzleflank said it was excellent to see how Dave had got into the character of a scruffy donkey and that he'd even done 'pretend stage farts' which 'showed such commitment to the role'.

'Um yes,' said Mira. 'Definitely pretend farts. Well done, Dave.'

Then Flo auditioned and repeated the only bits of her script Dave hadn't eaten – 'I'm so lonely' and 'Look at the sn' – in lots of different ways.

When everyone had auditioned they all sat back down and chatted, while Ms Dazzleflank looked through her notes.

Darcy went up to the front to speak to her,
but Mira couldn't hear what they were saying.
Mira fiddled with the corners of her script and
watched the drama teacher while Dave noisily
chomped on his mini doughnuts. She just hoped
they'd done enough. She REALLY wanted the
main part AND that Star of the Show medal!

CHAPTER FOUR
The Rehearsals Begin

Ms Dazzleflank was going to put the cast list on the Unicorn School noticeboard by the end of the day, which seemed to Mira like a very long time to wait.

Luckily, all of their lessons had a fun festive theme. Their cookery teacher, Mr Nosebag, showed them how to make Christmas cookies and Decorated Festive Carrots. Dave sneakily ate quite a few of the cookies but generously left the carrots.

Then it was PE, where they did ice skating

on the frozen swimming pool. Dave kept licking the ice as if it was a giant ice lolly until Miss Hind told him to stop it. Finally it was Maths, where they were doing Fun Festive Times Tables, which were actually just normal times tables but everyone was wearing Christmas hats. Dave fell asleep (Mira didn't really blame him for that one).

And then FINALLY it was the end of the day and time to find out their roles in the play!

Ms Dazzleflank pinned a sheet of names to the noticeboard and Class Red crowded round.

Mira was stuck at the back and couldn't see the sheet.

She tried to peer round people's heads.

'That's so cool, Seb – you get to look after the eighty million horses!' said Freya.

'I wonder how they're going to get them all on the stage,' said Tamsin thoughtfully.

Darcy flicked through the script for mentions of Magical Sprite 2 and then decided she'd rather play the role of Grand High Wizard, which she'd just made up.

'I'M THE NARRATOR??' shouted Raheem in terror.

'Oh that's perfect,' said Ms Dazzleflank. 'Do it just as loudly as that on the night.'

'BUT –' spluttered Raheem. The teacher held up her hand.

'You must save your voice,' she said. 'Your friend told me just how wonderfully you read aloud to your sister in the car park this morning.' Ms Dazzleflank pointed at Darcy, who grinned at Raheem and gave him a double thumbs-up. Raheem looked at Darcy with an expression that was half shock and half fury.

Eventually Mira got to the front and could see the list of names. *There* was the all-important role...

MAGICAL SPRITE 2: Darcy
SNOW CHILD &
    SNOW UNICORN:
Flo and Sparkles

'SPARKLES!' screamed Flo, who was standing next to her. 'We're the Snow Unicorn and Child!'

Mira felt like her heart had plummeted all the way into her shoes. The class surrounded Flo to congratulate her. Mira joined in, blinking to make sure she didn't cry.

Everyone was wandering away from the noticeboard now, chatting about their roles. Mira looked at the list again. I bet I'm Magical Sprite 3 or something, she thought glumly.

But she wasn't Magical Sprite 3.

'Ms Dazzleflank?' Mira said uncertainly.

'Hmm?' said the teacher, who was turning to go.

'I don't think . . . Dave and I are on the list?'

Ms Dazzleflank scanned the sheet of names.

'Er . . . yes, of course,' she said, looking through her notes. 'Of course, Mira and Dave are . . .' She picked up a script and flicked through it. 'The *very* important roles of . . . Worm and Pebble!'

She wrote '*Mira and Dave: Worm and Pebble*' in pencil at the bottom of the cast list.

Mira sighed. She tried to pick up her bag, but Dave was lying on it and he had gone into one of his deep sleeps where he was impossible to move. Like a rock, thought Mira. Or . . .

'A pebble!' she said out loud. 'You're right, Dave. Sometimes it's the tortoise that wins the race. Sometimes it's the Worm that gets the medal. We're going to be the BEST Worm and Pebble there has ever been!'

∪∪∪

The next morning it was time for their first play rehearsal, so Class Red headed to the REALM OF THE THEATRE right after breakfast.

Class Yellow brought in the scenery they'd made the previous day, and set it up around the room. The real performance would be outside, around the big special Christmas tree, but for now they put a little pot of cress to mark where the tree would go.

'I basically painted that whole castle,' said Rani, stepping over Mira, who was lying on the floor being a worm. 'Are the Worm and the Pebble even *in* the story? I don't remember them at all.'

Mira ignored her sister and kept wiggling. After all, who said that the winner of the Star of the Show medal couldn't be a worm?

When Class Yellow had left, Ms Dazzleflank got all of Class Red to stand in a circle.

'You are no longer Class Red,' she said. 'You are Energy. You are Emotion. You are The Play. You are the THEATRE. We shall begin. FEEL your way, and remember that in theatre there is no right or wrong. There is only truth.'

Flo stepped to the front and took a deep breath.

'I AM SO LONELY I WISH I HAD SOME FRIENDS SHE POINTS AT THE CASTLE OH THE PRINCE HAS ALL HE COULD EVER WANT –'

'Your energy is wonderful, Flo,' interrupted Ms Dazzleflank, 'but let's just give the lines a chance to breathe and try not to say the stage directions.'

'I'M SORRY MS DAZZLEFLANK I'M JUST SO EXCITED AND I THOUGHT THERE WASN'T ANY RIGHT OR WRONG IN THEATRE.'

'Yes,' said Ms Dazzleflank. 'Of course. Now I think we'll move on to a later bit in the script. Can we have our Narrator?'

Raheem shuffled forward. Darcy and Mira gave him a thumbs up. He breathed in and out a few times, and then he held his script in front of his face and began to speak.

'Once upon a time there was a girl.'

Unfortunately he was speaking so quietly that no one could hear him. As they went through the scene, despite all the teacher's encouragement, Raheem was so nervous he could only whisper. Flo, meanwhile, continued to scream all her lines.

Darcy managed to get the Grand High Wizard into quite a lot of the scenes by inventing reasons to come on, such as asking the Prince if he wanted her to magic up a new crown, or because she thought she might have left her wand and her hat in the forest somewhere.

But, brilliantly, because the Worm and the Pebble weren't mentioned in the script, Ms Dazzleflank said that they could appear in every scene! So in every scene Mira wiggled away on the floor, and Dave was excelling at his role as the Pebble because all he had to do was not move – which meant he could have a doze.

When they finished the run-through, the class got back into their circle again, around

Ms Dazzleflank's desk because she'd had to have a little sit-down.

'Wonderful, really magical,' she said, having a big gulp of tea.

'THANKS,' screamed Flo.

'It's all going to be wonderful,' said the teacher faintly. 'And Raheem, I just know you will find your voice for the big day.'

Raheem nodded, but he didn't look so sure.

CHAPTER FIVE
The Christmas Quest

As she took the morning register Miss Glitterhorn told Class Red that it was almost time for their quest! Everyone cheered except Dave, who had fallen asleep face-down under the desk with his bum poking up in the air.

'Now then children,' said Miss Glitterhorn. 'As you know, your performance of *The Legend of the Snow Unicorn* will take place under the special Christmas tree in the paddock.'

The class all nodded, except Flo, who had thought they would be performing under the

little pot of cress.

'But can anyone see the problem?' asked Miss Glitterhorn. 'Yes, Darcy?'

'There isn't a Christmas tree in the paddock, Miss Glitterhorn,' said Darcy.

'Exactly!' said Miss Glitterhorn. 'Our quest shall be to journey into the Fearsome Forest and return with the perfect Christmas tree.'

Class Red were *very* excited about this quest.

'We have to make sure it is literally the most perfect tree in the whole forest,' said Tamsin.

'It needs to have LOADS of pine needles, and smell all Christmassy,' said Seb.

'And it needs to be MASSIVE,' said Darcy.

Everyone nodded in agreement.

Miss Glitterhorn told them that when they found the perfect tree, they would need to say the Perfect Tree Spell. The spell was on a scroll, which Miss Glitterhorn gave to Darcy, as she was going to be the quest leader.

Then Miss Glitterhorn went round checking that everyone had packed what they needed for the quest – notebook, water bottle, snack. Raheem was bringing a spare of everything, plus extra socks, in his emergency bumbag.

'Raheem, what are you strapping to your back?' said Miss Glitterhorn.

'Metre sticks!' Raheem said. 'For measuring the tree. So we can make sure it's the perfect size. I thought I'd bring five?'

'I think two will be quite enough,' said Miss Glitterhorn.

A few moments later, Class Red went outside, mounted their unicorns and rode towards the Fearsome Forest. The sun shone brightly in the clear sky, making the snow sparkle even more. Mira gave a little shiver, not sure if it was the cold or the excitement. The crunching of hooves in the snow and the sight of everyone's breath in the chilly air somehow made this quest even more magical.

They made their way across the paddock, the unicorns picking up their feet more than usual as their hooves sank into the snow. They seemed grateful for their cosy Christmas jumpers. Mira had brought one of her dad's jumpers from home

that had a big picture of a doughnut on it
and 'DOUGHNUT WORRY, BE HAPPY',
which she thought was perfect for Dave. He
seemed very happy in it, even though it was
a bit big.

Mira trotted along on Dave and gave him a
scratch behind the ears. Dave did a happy fart.
There really was nothing like going on a quest
with your UBFF!

'Oh look,' said Miss Glitterhorn. 'There are
some lovely trees just by the entrance to the
forest. How convenient!'

'Hmm,' said Darcy, getting to the clump of pine
trees and inspecting them. 'They *are* nice – but
are they the best we can do?'

'Well I think that one is excellent,' said Miss Glitterhorn, pointing to a tree at the corner of the clump that was slightly taller than the others.

'It's very green,' said Tamsin. 'But I feel like the perfect tree would be even greener?'

Seb trotted over to the tree on Firework and sniffed it. 'It doesn't smell Christmassy enough,' he said.

The other children agreed that they could do better than those trees and they needed to go further into the forest. Miss Glitterhorn gave a loud sigh.

As they headed into the forest, the branches of the tall trees hung above their heads, casting shadows on the snowy path. The forest was quiet, apart from the occasional sound of snow sliding

off branches on to the ground.

Next to Mira and Dave, Raheem's unicorn Brave was flicking his head from side to side. Mira knew he was keeping an eye out for sparkle spiders, which he was really scared of.

Raheem was calming Brave down like he always did. But Mira saw that Raheem seemed distracted, and even more anxious than usual.

Miss Glitterhorn kept pointing out 'perfectly good trees', but Class Red felt that perfectly good wasn't *perfect*, and there must be so many great trees they hadn't seen. So further into the forest they went.

After about an hour, Miss Glitterhorn looked at her watch. 'We really need to get back,' she said.

'So I am afraid that the next perfectly good tree we see will need to be –'

'FOUND IT!' came shouts from up ahead. It was Darcy and Flo.

'Thank goodness,' sighed Miss Glitterhorn.

Miss Glitterhorn and her unicorn, Heathcliff, were at the back of the group with Mira and Dave. Dave's little legs meant he was often a lot slower than the other unicorns.

'Now we just need to chant the Perfect Tree Spell,' called Miss Glitterhorn as they approached the clearing where the shouts had come from. 'The spell will pop the tree out of the ground and a couple of the unicorns can carry it back and – oh my word, it's enormous!'

Mira looked up as she entered the clearing. The tree was beautifully bushy, with lots of shiny needles and a thick trunk, and lots of space underneath for them to perform. There was no denying it – it was the Perfect Tree.

And it was also massive.

'I think we'll keep looking, Class Red –' began Miss Glitterhorn, but she was too late. The class were all chanting the Perfect Tree Spell.

The massive tree creaked and groaned and began to tilt. Children and unicorns scattered. The tree hit the ground with a thundering crash that sent shudders throughout the forest. A heap of snow slid from a nearby branch and landed neatly on Miss Glitterhorn's head.

∪ ∪ ∪

76

Class Red moved slowly back through the Fearsome Forest in the direction of Unicorn School. Miss Glitterhorn had brought some harnesses, and so all the unicorns were hooked up to the Perfect Massive Tree and were pulling it along slowly like reindeer pulling a sleigh.

Mira and Dave were walking next to Raheem and Brave, with Darcy and Star on the other side.

'Are you feeling okay, Raheem?' Mira asked.

Raheem fiddled with Brave's mane. 'It's just . . . it's just this play,' he said. 'You know how our parents are coming to see it?'

Mira nodded. She'd rung her mum and dad that morning and shouted, 'I'm the Worm!' They were a bit confused at first, but they said

they were so pleased for her, especially when she
told them she was appearing in every scene!

'My mum's SO excited that I'm going to be
the narrator,' said Raheem. 'She's told all her
friends. And my sister's excited too, even though
she can't come and watch. Mum sent me a
picture she drew.'

He showed Mira and Darcy the picture on
his phone. It was a drawing of Raheem,

and underneath it said
MY BROTHER –
SOOPER NARAYTOR.

'Mum's going to film it
all for her,' said Raheem.
'I just think they'll be
so disappointed when they
realise I can't even speak
in front of people.'

'I'm sure you'll be able to do it,' said Mira.
'Your sister thinks so too!'

Raheem looked even more miserable. 'The only
time I ever enjoy reading out loud is when I read
stories to Tia. But the thought of speaking in front
of EVERYONE makes my tummy feel funny.'

'It's just volume,' said Darcy. 'We'll turn you up!'

'I don't know what that means,' said Raheem.

'You're fine saying the lines,' explained Darcy. 'So we just need to turn your volume up. I'll show you.'

'Okay,' said Raheem, looking over at Mira, who shrugged.

'Repeat after me,' said Darcy. 'Hooves. Mane. Tail. Horn. What does that make? Unicorn!'

'Hooves. Mane. Tail. Horn. What does that make? Unicorn,' said Raheem quietly.

'Hooves. Mane. Tail. Horn. What does that make? Unicorn!' said Darcy, a little bit louder this time.

Raheem repeated it, and Darcy said it again, and they kept going back and forth, getting a bit louder each time. Mira joined in with Darcy. Their unicorns

began to snort and whinny along, and even Dave
farted in time with the chant. Raheem was getting
so into the song that he didn't seem to have noticed
that his voice had got louder and louder.

'Hooves. Mane. Tail. Horn. What
does that make? UNICORN!'

Raheem yelled at the top of his voice. Dave
accompanied him with a fart so deafening it
sounded like a giant explosion. It was so loud that
all the unicorns were startled and some of the
children screamed. Everyone stopped abruptly,
and Miss Glitterhorn nearly fell off Heathcliff.
The trees around them shook.

Then, in the distance, they heard a rumbling
sound. The ground began to tremble. Just ahead

RRUUMMBBLEE

of them, a huge pile of snow tumbled down from a rocky outcrop.

'A load of snow has fallen on to the path. It's completely blocked!' called Jake from the front of the group.

Mira peered over the heads of her classmates and their unicorns. A gigantic mound of snow rose up in front of them. It was almost as high as the top of the tall trees.

How were they going to get back?

CHAPTER SIX
A Snowy Surprise

Class Red were silent as they unhooked the harnesses from their unicorns. They were right on the edge of the forest and SO close to the school, but in order to get back they were going to have to climb up and over the giant mound of snow. There was no way the unicorns could pull the Perfect Massive Tree as well, so they'd have to leave it behind.

'Is everyone ready to go?' said Miss Glitterhorn.

'Nearly!' said Mira. She was struggling to get

Dave out of his harness, which had got tangled in the arms of Mira's dad's jumper. Raheem went to help.

Darcy rode Star over to their teacher. 'Miss Glitterhorn,' she said. 'We just want to have a moment with the tree. To say goodbye.'

Star walked solemnly over to the Perfect Massive Tree. The other children and unicorns followed, their heads bowed.

Mira sighed as she struggled with the harness. She wished they weren't going back empty-handed. Just on the other side of the giant snow mound, everything would be set up for the Snow Unicorn celebrations. She thought she could just about make out the sound of cheerful

voices. And there was a smell in the air . . . it was very faint, but – yes, she could definitely smell hot chocolate.

There was a snort. Dave's ears pricked up and his nostrils twitched. And Mira saw a crazed look enter his eyes as he inhaled the sweet chocolatey smell too.

'Um, Dave . . .' she said.

Dave shot forward, but he was still attached to his harness. The harness rope went tight. The rope strained. Dave's little legs were moving so fast that showers of snow flew up around him.

And then the Perfect Massive Tree began to move. Slowly at first, and then it started sliding quickly through the snow.

'GRAB ON!' shouted Mira, scrambling on to Dave's back.

All the children and unicorns leaped towards the tree and held on to branches and harness ropes. Darcy ended up clinging to the trunk. Miss Glitterhorn was holding on to Heathcliff's leg.

As Dave began to climb the snow mound, he slowed down a bit.

But then the other unicorns surged forward
as they all caught the scent of the hot chocolate.
Some managed to slip back into their harnesses.
Others pulled the ropes with their teeth. And
now the Perfect Massive Tree began to move
up the icy slope!

Raheem bumped along behind Mira with his
arms and legs wrapped around Brave and his eyes
squeezed shut. He was saying something, but
Mira couldn't hear him over the whooshing of
the tree through the snow.

'What?' she called to him.

Raheem said it again, but Mira still couldn't hear. They were approaching the top of the snow mound now. Mira gasped as she saw the glittering white hills and fields laid out beneath them. She could see for miles. The snowy mountains were behind them, and ahead were the snow-topped turrets of Unicorn School. It was beautiful!

'What did you say, Raheem?' she asked again.

'I SAID I'M NEVER YELLING AGAIN!' Raheem yelled.

The far-off rumbling noise returned. This time, it kept going. Mira turned back to see a huge white cloud of snow tearing down one of the magical mountains that surrounded the forest. It was getting bigger and bigger.

'AVALANCHE!!' Mira shouted.

Everyone screamed. Mira felt her stomach leap into her throat as Dave dipped downwards. He was running down the other side of the snow mound now. The Perfect Massive Tree sleigh began to gain speed.

'THIS IS SO MUCH FUN!' whooped Darcy from her position on the trunk.

'If you think DYING is FUN!' howled Raheem.

The tree sleigh was moving faster and faster, sending up sprays of powdery whiteness. But behind them the giant cloud of snow was getting closer.

'It's closing in on us!' shouted Freya.

Mira looked around desperately. The rumbling was so loud now it was drowning everything else out. They needed to go faster. What could she do? She thought frantically about all the things in her rucksack. Was there anything she could use?

Wait . . .

'Raheem, give me your metre sticks!' Mira called, twisting round.

Raheem's eyes snapped open in surprise. He carefully reached into his backpack, grabbed the measuring sticks and threw them to Mira.

Before Mira could think about it too much, she squeezed as hard as she could with her knees and made a lunge for the sticks. Her fingers closed around them. With all her strength, she

threw them down on the snow in front of Dave's hooves. He did a little jump, so that his hooves landed on the long, thin sticks.

Now Dave was skiing. He zoomed across the snow, with the tree sleigh speeding up behind him. They kept just ahead of the avalanche, but it was getting closer and closer . . . Unicorn School was right in front of them and Mira could see pupils and teachers gathered in the paddock, standing around tables with big urns on them . . .

Too late! The avalanche crashed around them. Class Red shot into the air . . . and Mira braced herself, squeezing her eyes tight shut.

But they didn't hit the ground like she was expecting.

Mira opened her eyes.

They were above the avalanche, surfing the rolling snow like a wave.

Mira saw the panicked faces in the paddock as Class Red and the Perfect Massive Tree surfed towards them. But the avalanche began dipping and slowing. The rumbling around them grew quieter and the wave grew smaller and smaller.

★ A Snowy Surprise ★

Finally it dumped them gently in the paddock, next to the table of hot chocolate. Children and unicorns tumbled from the tree and into the snow.

Mira climbed to her feet and brushed the snow out of her eyes. Dave was lying under one of the urns, mouth wide open as a stream of hot chocolate poured into his throat.

CHAPTER SEVEN
Party Preparations

The next morning the whole school was out in the paddock again, helping to transform it for the Snow Unicorn celebrations.

The paddock was decorated with lanterns, with stalls of different Christmas treats around the edge. Signs pointed to the ice-skating rink (the frozen swimming pool), and the Perfect Massive Christmas Tree stood proudly in the middle. It might have lost a few needles on its journey across the snow, but it still looked pretty impressive. All the other classes crowded

round to admire it and to ask about the story

of the avalanche, so Class Red were pleased

they'd risked certain death to bring it back (Miss

Glitterhorn felt differently).

Once they'd hung red and green tinsel all around the fence and put the Decorated Festive Carrots under the tree for the Snow Unicorn, Class Red were allowed to wander round the different stalls. Mira decided to practise for the play. She'd already made Dave go through their scenes quite a few (seventeen) times before breakfast, but once more couldn't hurt!

She looked around for her unicorn, and saw that he was still by the tree. Class Orange were hanging chocolate decorations on the branches, and each time they put one on Dave would pop up and eat it. Mira quickly led him away.

'Right, Dave — let's go through all the scenes again!' she began.

Dave gave her a sly look, and then fell sideways in the snow and started snoring.

'Dave!' Mira said into his ear.

He opened one eye and then scrunched it shut again.

Hmm, Mira thought.

She made a little ball out of the powdery snow and threw it at the snoozing unicorn. But Dave opened his eyes at the last minute, caught it in his mouth and spat it back. Mira made another snowball and threw it at Dave, but Dave did the same thing. Then Dave made a big snowball and threw it at Mira. She squealed as some of the snow went inside her coat.

'Okay,' Mira spluttered. 'We can have a quick

snowball fight, but then we are rehearsing the

pla— ARGGHHH!'

Another snowball hit her on the top of the

head. Mira forgot all thoughts of the play as

she started making a huge snowball to take

her revenge.

As Mira and Dave ran around the tree, ducking and diving and throwing snowballs as quickly as they could, Mira was laughing so much she could hardly breathe. One of the snowballs hit Freya, who immediately made her own and threw it back. Soon all of Class Red joined in!

By the time Ms Dazzleflank appeared in the paddock, Class Red were soaking wet, freezing cold and very happy. And it was time for their final rehearsal. Class Yellow had set up the scenery and the stage, so it was going to be exactly like the real performance. This was the last chance to practise! Mira hoped that all the extra run-throughs they'd done would be enough. She desperately wanted that Star of the Show medal . . .

ᑌᑌᑌ

'How was the rehearsal, Class Red?' said Miss
Glitterhorn. The rehearsal was over and the rest
of the school and the teachers were joining Class
Red by the tree. It would soon be time for them
to leave their wishes for the Snow Unicorn!

'It was great!' said Flo. 'Ms Dazzleflank's just
gone off for a walk on her own to think about
how good it was.'

'It was a disaster,' said Jake. 'Flo still screams
all her lines, you can't hear Raheem at all, the
"Pebble" spends all its time eating and I've only
got two lines.'

'Just make up some more lines – that's what
I did,' said Darcy.

'Well, you know what they say,' said Miss

Glitterhorn. 'A bad last rehearsal means a brilliant performance!'

'What if it just means we're not very good?' said Raheem, looking worried.

Madame Shetland arrived by the tree to officially begin the wish-making. She asked for some volunteers to give out the wish sheets.

Mira was worried about her performance too. 'You have to stop eating on stage, Dave,' she said. 'Otherwise I'll – I mean we'll – never win the medal.'

Dave blinked at her and burped, which in Dave language could mean anything.

Mira looked over at the Perfect Massive Christmas Tree, where Class Blue were already

putting down their wishes. The tree decorations sparkled and the fairy lights twinkled, making patterns on the glittery snow.

'Here's your wish sheet,' said Mira's sister Rani, appearing beside her with a piece of paper and an envelope. 'Don't waste it on something rubbish.'

'Thanks!' said Mira, grabbing the wish sheet from Rani.

Next to Mira, Raheem was already writing his wish. She wondered if he was wishing to do a good job of his lines. Mira caught Raheem's eye and gave him an encouraging smile. He'd tried so hard in the rehearsal to speak louder.

Glancing at Darcy, Mira saw she was attaching a selfie of her and Star to her wish. One by one, all

the children from the other classes went to put their wishes under the tree. Raheem walked past looking more anxious than ever. Mira chewed her pen.

She turned back to her wish sheet. She knew exactly what her wish should be.

∪∪∪

Mira woke up on the morning of the Snow
Unicorn celebrations feeling more excited
than she'd ever been. It was the day of the play,
her mum and dad would see it, and afterwards
everyone was going to enjoy the fun with their
unicorns. And maybe, just maybe, they'd catch a
glimpse of the Snow Unicorn – and see if their
wishes had been granted!

The rest of Class Red were excited too,
except Raheem. And as they walked out into
the paddock, they saw some of the parents had
arrived already.

'THERE'S MY BOY!' shouted a voice.
A woman was waving and pointing to Raheem.

'Hi Mum!' Raheem said, waving back.

'Is your mum wearing a T-shirt with a picture of your face?' said Darcy.

'Yes. Yes she is,' said Raheem, his eyes wide.

'Actors!' called Ms Dazzleflank, throwing her arms in the air and staring into the distance. 'A spirit approaches!'

The class all looked round.

'Oh that's just Miss Hind,' said Freya, pointing at their PE teacher who was walking along the path. Miss Hind, who was always quite grumpy, scowled at them.

'No,' said Ms Dazzleflank. 'I meant the Spirit of Theatre. It is arriving to take hold of us, and light the dramatic fire.'

'It definitely is Miss Hind,' said Seb. 'I think she's putting out the mats for Festive Unicorn yoga.'

'Never mind,' said the drama teacher. 'Everyone close your eyes and focus on the voice within yourself.'

They were standing backstage behind the Perfect Massive Christmas Tree. Mira closed her eyes. She could hear the chatter of the parents and the other Unicorn School classes as they took their seats on the other side of the tree. And she could hear something else . . .

Crunch. Crunch. Crunch.

Mira tried to ignore it and focus on her inner Worm.

'Remember my three golden rules,' said Ms Dazzleflank. 'Believe. Be Brave. Is someone eating biscuits?'

'That's a weird third rule,' said Darcy.

Mira opened her eyes. Dave was already halfway through a plate of ginger unicorn-shaped biscuits that he must have swiped from one of the stalls.

'Dave!' She snatched the plate away, and then realised that Dave was hiding something else behind his back. 'What's that? A lunchbox! Why does a pebble need a lunchbox?!'

She made a grab for the lunchbox, but Dave dodged out of the way and stuck out his tongue. Mira narrowed her eyes. She was NOT going to let Dave's snacking ruin the play AND ruin her

chances of winning the Star of the Show medal!

Mira ran at Dave and rugby-tackled him. She tried to pin him to the ground so she could get the lunchbox, but he was too wriggly.

'Give . . . me . . . the . . . SNACKS!'

They rolled over and over in the snow. Every time Mira got hold of the lunchbox, Dave twisted it out of her grip. Mira made an extra big lunge. As Dave jerked the lunchbox away, it flew out of his hoof and tumbled along the snow. Mira and Dave both dived for it, but Mira was quicker.

'YES!' she cried triumphantly, waving the lunchbox above her head.

'MIRA AND DAVE!' thundered a voice. It was their head teacher, Madame Shetland.

Mira looked up. They'd rolled out from behind the stage and the audience could see them.

'Is this part of the show?' said one of the parents.

Someone started clapping, but then they stopped.

'Hi, darling!' called Mira's dad.

'Unicorn School Rule Number 67: no wrestling!' said Madame Shetland, as she ushered them off the stage.

Dave snorted. He took the lunchbox out of Mira's hands and put it down carefully at the side of the stage, and then stood with his back to Mira. Mira folded her arms.

'Wonderful energy from the Worm and the Pebble!' said Ms Dazzleflank. 'You must channel it into your performance. Now, let us begin!'

CHAPTER EIGHT
Showtime!

The play opened with all the characters on stage, walking around and miming being in a forest, as Ms Dazzleflank had said this would 'set the scene'.

They could immediately hear Raheem's mum. 'THERE'S MY BABY!' and 'GREAT JOB, SWEETIE!' Raheem shuffled nearer the back of the stage.

A trumpet blast from the Class Indigo orchestra signalled the end of the first scene.

Mira wiggled to the side of the stage, and Dave rolled after her. They still hadn't made eye

contact since the play began. Mira was feeling a bit bad about wrestling him for the snacks.

Freya the Prince appeared at the castle window, and Flo marched out in front of the castle door. Her unicorn Sparkles followed her.

'Excellent weird scabby old donkey costume,' said someone in the audience.

Raheem stepped forward to the front of the stage. His mum gave him a round of applause.

Raheem swallowed, and took a deep breath.

'Once upon a time there was a girl.'

People in the audience leaned forward, trying to hear him.

Raheem cleared his throat and tried again, but all that came out was a whisper.

'I can't hear anything he's saying,' said a boy from Class Green, who was quickly shushed by a teacher.

'You can do it, Raheem,' Mira muttered under her breath. 'Once upon a time there was a girl, and the girl . . .' Then she realised something. The Worm and the Pebble were in the background of every scene, plus Mira knew ALL of the lines. And that gave her an idea . . .

Mira wiggled behind Dave, so she wouldn't be visible from the audience. Then she started to speak.

'Once upon a time there was a girl.'

Raheem turned to look at her.

'And the girl lived in a tiny cottage,' Mira continued.

Raheem grinned at Mira. He'd worked out her plan! He turned to face the audience, and began to say his lines, just as quietly as before, but this time Mira was saying them too so the audience could hear.

They reached the end of his first speech and his mum cheered wildly. Mira saw that she was filming it all. That gave her another idea . . .

'I AM SO LONELY I WISH I HAD SOME FRIENDS THE CHILD POINTS AT THE DONKEY I ONLY HAVE THIS DONKEY,' yelled Flo at the top of her voice.

Soon it was the interval, and Mira decided to put her plan into action. She saw Madame Shetland waiting at the snow-floss stand. Mira hoped she would have enough time, but just in case, she went to find Darcy, who was waiting in the wings and adjusting her Wizard's hat.

'Darcy, when you go back on, can you make your scene a bit longer so that there's a gap

before Raheem's next bit?'

'Of COURSE!' said Darcy gleefully. 'Leave it with me.'

Mira saw Dave looking at her in confusion. 'I'll be back in a moment, Dave!' she said.

∪∪∪

By the time Mira got back, the second half had begun – but Raheem hadn't come on yet and Darcy and Jake were on stage. Freya whispered to Mira that Jake had been annoyed at first when Darcy had interrupted his scene by shouting, 'I am the Grand High Wizard and I am going to take over the world!' but now he was enjoying making up lines and pretending to be the Big Evil Wizard who was going to defeat her.

Mira headed back on to the stage. As she wiggled through the wings, Jake and Darcy were being dragged off by Ms Dazzleflank in the middle of doing a Wizard dance.

Then Raheem walked on stage. Mira got back into position just in time, as Raheem looked over nervously to check she was there.

'One day the girl was standing outside the castle when it started to snow,' said Mira, and Raheem mouthed along.

'LOOK AT THE SN,' shouted Flo.

'The snow made the world even more . . .' Mira stopped, and Raheem looked over at her. She pointed into the crowd, and Raheem turned back. His mum was on the front row now, and

standing next to her was . . .

'Tia!' said Raheem.

'Big bro!' shouted Tia. She waved and Raheem
waved back.

'The snow made the world even more . . .' Mira
started again.

'. . . magical than usual,' said Raheem clearly.
'And as the girl walked through the forest, she
had the feeling that something quite special
might happen that day.'

He was saying the lines, and everyone could
hear! Raheem continued to speak clearly, always
staring straight at his little sister, who grinned
back at him.

Mira felt so happy as she wiggled back into her position. She'd managed to persuade Madame Shetland to bend the rules just this once, and let Tia come to the show so that Raheem could enjoy his role. Raheem's mum had raced back through the portal to get her!

The play carried on, and the audience were loving it. They cheered each time Jake and Darcy sneaked back on stage. And they booed and hissed when the Prince chased them away. When it was revealed that the Weird Scabby Old Donkey was magic, a man (who Mira thought was Flo and Freya's dad) stood on his seat and shouted, 'YAY!' Madame Shetland asked him to sit down.

But then, when they got to the part where the Donkey told the Girl to go away and think about her wish, Raheem stopped.

Oh no! He's got stage fright again! Mira thought. But Raheem raised his hand.

'Now, this is a really exciting part of the story,' he said. 'And there's someone here who tells it better than anyone I know. Everyone please give a big clap for . . . the Worm!'

Mira stared at him open-mouthed as the crowd burst into applause.

'Come on!' said Raheem.

Mira felt something on her elbow and realised that Dave was giving her a nudge with his nose. She wiggled up to the front of the stage.

'This was the bit of the story you got to in the drama lesson,' said Raheem. 'So I thought it would be nice for you to get to finish it.'

THE LEGEND OF THE SNOW UNICORN (part 2):

The Girl walked around having a think about what her wish should be. As she was thinking, she walked past the castle and she thought she would have another look, just to make definitely sure that she did want that wish. But when she looked in the castle window again, she saw that the Prince's toys were actually games for two people so he couldn't play them, and all the eighty million horses did stuff together and didn't involve the

Prince, and also it was his birthday and no one had shown up. The Donkey was right! thought the Girl and then just like that the Donkey EXPLODED out of the air and appeared on the path in front of her. And the Girl said, 'I have a new wish. My wish is that the Prince could have some friends of his own.' The Donkey smiled and he granted the wish with a clop of his hooves and loads of peasant kids from the village turned up to the party and the Prince was like, 'Argh they're all dirty and they are mucking up my toys!' but secretly he was pleased. And all the horses turned into unicorns. And the Girl was looking through the window and she thought, that's so nice, I'm glad I changed my wish. And she turned to walk away and go back home

to her sad life. BUT then the Prince came running out of the castle shouting, 'WAIT!' and he caught up with her and he said, 'You can come into the castle and play with the unicorns.' Which is all the Girl had ever wanted, so she said 'Yay!' and ran towards the castle. But then she remembered something. The Donkey was turning to go and the Girl was like, 'What about you?' And the Donkey said, 'I just live alone in a magic hole.'

So the Girl said, 'I wish you had a special friend.' And then the Donkey transformed and he turned white and glittery as snow and a horn grew at the top of his head. And he said, 'I am the Snow Unicorn. I'll be your new Unicorn Best Friend Forever.'

When Mira finished the story the audience was on its feet and the applause was deafening. Class Red did five bows and still everyone was clapping and cheering!

'Hey, look – Dave's still in character!' said Raheem as they finally left the stage.

Sure enough, the plump little unicorn was now curled up and barely moving. Just like a pebble.

Mira looked over and grinned. 'I'll bet you anything he's asleep.'

Dave gave a massive snore.

'Come on, Dave,' said Mira, giving him a shove. It was time to go and enjoy the Snow Unicorn celebrations, and she didn't want to do it without her UBFF by her side!

CHAPTER NINE
Wishes, Gifts and Festive Fun!

'Have you tried the snow-floss?' said Darcy.
'Yum-arama.'

'Can I have some?' said a voice from under
Raheem's arm. Tia wanted her brother to take her
round every single stall so she didn't miss a THING.

It was dusk now and the paddock was lit by the
lanterns and by the twinkling fairy lights on the
Perfect Massive Christmas Tree.

'The ice-skating is so fun!' called Flo, running
over in a strange, lolloping way because she still

had the ice skates on.

'I'm not doing that,' said Raheem firmly.

'I am!' said Tia, and she ran off with Flo.

'This is NOT a drill,' said Darcy. 'There are presents under the tree!'

The friends all looked at each other. That could only mean one thing. The Snow Unicorn had visited and the Christmas wishes had been granted!

The children crowded round the tree, searching for the presents with their names on. Flo unwrapped her present, which was a chocolate-making kit. 'My wish came true! Now I can have chocolate forever!' she whooped.

Freya, who had wished she could fly, was super-excited to unwrap a hoverboard. There was one for her unicorn, Princess, too.

Seb unwrapped rainbow hair-dye and a pair of

shades. 'I'm going to be just like Firework!' he said.

'Does it wash out?' said his mum.

'There's nothing with my name on,' said Darcy, looking confused.

'Excuse me?' said a voice. It was a girl from Class Orange, with her friends standing nervously behind.

'Yes?' said Darcy, still looking around for her present.

'Can we have your autograph?' said the girl.

'Can I have a selfie?' called a boy standing at the back of the group.

'Uh, sure?' said Darcy.

'We just think you're SO amazing,' said the girl. 'We've already learnt the Wizard dance.'

And then Darcy realised that there was a long line of people waiting to talk to her. There were children from all the other classes, a couple of parents and one of the teachers.

'Darcy, you're famous!' said Raheem, grinning.

'I'm NEVER washing my hand again!' said one boy after Darcy had high-fived him.

'Aren't you going to have a look under the tree?' said Raheem to Mira as they left Darcy talking to her fans.

'My present's not under there,' said Mira.

'I don't think mine is either,' said Raheem. 'I wished that my sister could visit me at Unicorn School, and she has!'

It was time to award the Star of the Show

medal, so they returned to the seats by the stage. This time Class Red sat in the audience with their parents.

'You were a brilliant worm, darling!' said Mira's mum, and her dad gave her a hug and a kiss on the head.

'You were *quite* good,' said Rani, and Mira sat down beside her sister, a big smile on her face.

'This medal goes to someone who has given a real stand-out performance in our *Legend of the Snow Unicorn* play,' said Madame Shetland from the stage. 'And while *all* the performances were very special . . .'

'DARCY! DARCY! DARCY!' shouted Darcy's fans.

'. . . this person overcame his fear, created a special moment for his friend, and for us all,' said Madame Shetland. 'The Star of the Show medal goes to . . . Raheem!'

The crowd erupted into cheers. The loudest cheers came from Raheem's mum, of course. She covered Raheem with kisses while he tried to wriggle away.

Raheem looked over at Mira worriedly. He knew how much Mira had wanted the Star of the Show medal. But Mira grinned back at him. She'd changed her wish at the last minute, wishing that Raheem would find his voice and enjoy the play. And although she was sorry not to have won the special medal, she'd still had an

absolutely brilliant time AND got to play one of the main parts, at least for a bit!

'And now it's time to party!' said a boy from Class Violet, who had set up some DJ decks on the stage.

'Yes, quite,' said Madame Shetland, and Mira realised that she'd put a little Santa hat on.

The head teacher asked everyone to help move the chairs to the side to create a dancefloor. The speakers began to blast out Christmas songs.

'YES!' shouted Rani, running to the middle of the dancefloor. Darcy followed her, and so did Darcy's fans, and they all did the Wizard dance.

'Hey, wait! There's another present under the tree,' said Freya. She picked it up. 'Oh, actually it's

a lunchbox,' she said in surprise. 'It's for you, Mira.'

Mira took the box from Freya. It was very familiar, except for one thing – it had ribbon around it and a tag that said, *MiRA*.

Mira looked at Dave, who gazed at the ground and started scuffing his hoof in the snow.

She untied the ribbon and opened the box.

Inside was something round, made of silver foil with more ribbon. It was a home-made medal! And on the medal it said *MiRA No. 1*.

Raheem grinned at Mira. 'I think Dave made you your own special medal.'

Dave shrugged and scuffed his hoof again. So that was why he'd tried so hard to keep her away from

the lunchbox! Mira looked at her plump, grumpy, naughty UBFF and she thought she might cry.

'Dave,' said Mira. 'It's the best present ever.'

'Awesome medal!' said Darcy, wheeling over. 'Hey, and this is the best Christmas song!'

The friends and their unicorns all danced in a circle and sang at the top of their voices.

'All I want for Christmas is U-nicorn!'

∪ ∪ ∪

'Brrrr,' said Mira's dad as they all walked through the snow towards the landing haystack. 'It's very chilly now. If only *someone* hadn't borrowed my lovely warm doughnut jumper . . .'

They all glanced at Dave, who looked around and whistled. Everyone laughed.

'I'll just say bye to Dave,' said Mira.

As her parents walked on ahead, Mira turned around to say goodbye to her UBFF – and noticed something glinting in the snow by her foot.

She bent down. It was a scroll, tied with a glittery gold ribbon.

Mira loosened the ribbon and unrolled the scroll. Something was tied to one end of the ribbon. It was two tiny glass tree decorations – a girl and a unicorn! Dave nosed the figures and Mira popped one on the end of his horn and put the other one carefully in her pocket.

Then she read out the words on the scroll:

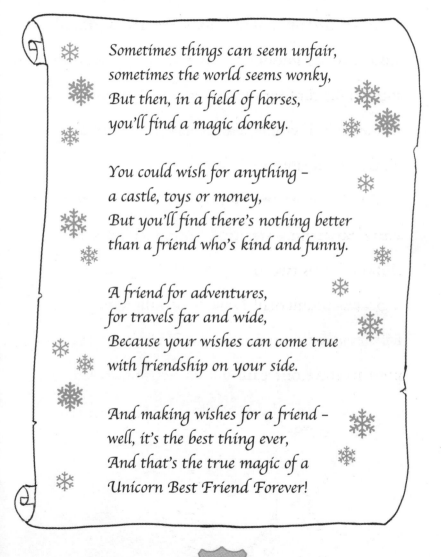

Sometimes things can seem unfair,
sometimes the world seems wonky,
But then, in a field of horses,
you'll find a magic donkey.

You could wish for anything –
a castle, toys or money,
But you'll find there's nothing better
than a friend who's kind and funny.

A friend for adventures,
for travels far and wide,
Because your wishes can come true
with friendship on your side.

And making wishes for a friend –
well, it's the best thing ever,
And that's the true magic of a
Unicorn Best Friend Forever!

Mira turned back to her UBFF and gave him a huge hug. A special message from the Snow Unicorn! She felt full of festive joy and happiness. Although it was always a *bit* sad saying goodbye to Dave, they'd had another brilliant adventure, and she knew she'd be back at Unicorn School soon.

'Bye Dave,' she said with a smile, giving him a huge hug and scratching him behind his ears. 'Merry Christmas!'

Dave cocked his head on side, the glass ornament tinkling. And as Mira raced off to join her family, Dave let off a final festive fart that echoed all around the paddock.

CHRISTMAS COOKIES

Ask a grown-up to help!

Dave the naughtiest unicorn LOVES all the delicious food there is to eat at Christmas time! Here's a special recipe for Mr Nosebag's Christmassy gingerbread cookies. This makes enough for around 14 cookies. Make sure you have a grown-up to help!

Ingredients

300g plain flour
1 teaspoon bicarbonate of soda
2 teaspoons ground ginger
½ teaspoon ground cinnamon
½ teaspoon ground nutmeg
125g unsalted butter
100g soft light brown sugar
3 tablespoons golden syrup

Equipment

A big bowl
2 baking sheets
Baking paper to line sheets
A selection of cookie cutters
A rolling pin

Preheat the oven to 180°C, or gas mark 4. In a big bowl, combine the flour, bicarbonate of soda, ginger, cinnamon and nutmeg.

Ask your grown-up to help you melt the butter, sugar and golden syrup in a pan over a low heat. Stir until the sugar melts, then add it to the flour mixture. Stir the mixture until this becomes a stiff dough, then cut the dough in half.

Take your two sheets of baking paper and place on a work surface. Place half of the dough on each sheet. Using your rolling pin, roll out the dough to around 5mm thick. Then start to cut out your cookie shapes using a cookie cutter of your choice!

Continue to cut out shapes until all your dough has been used up.

Carefully place the baking paper on to the baking sheets with your cookies in place.

Ask your grown-up to place these in the oven for 12-15 minutes, until the cookies are lightly golden.

Ask your grown-up to take the cookies out of the oven and leave to cool on a wire rack.

Once cool, ice the gingerbread cookies if you like – or decorate with sweets and sprinkles!

CHRISTMAS JOKES

Who delivers Christmas presents to cats and dogs?
Santa Paws!

How do snowmen get around?
They ride an icicle

What do you get if you cross a Christmas tree with an apple?
A pineapple

Which unicorn lives in space?
The moon-icorn!

What do you get if you cross a bell with a skunk?
Jingle Smells

What do unicorns say when they kiss?
Ouch!

What happened to the tiny unicorn?
He grew-nicorn

Look out for more brilliant
adventures with Dave and Mira!

The Naughtiest Unicorn

The Naughtiest Unicorn at Sports Day

The Naughtiest Unicorn and the School Disco